DAVE

Pigeon (Kittens)

Dave Pigeon's book on how
to raise a bunch of kittens
when you're a pigeon

By
Dave Pigeon, Skipper,
Swapna Haddow
and
Sheena Dempsey,
all of whom know absolutely
nothing about kittens

faber

First published in 2023
by Faber and Faber Limited
The Bindery, 51 Hatton Garden
London, EC1N 8HN
faber.co.uk

Designed by Faber and Faber
Printed and bound in the UK by
CPI Group (UK) Ltd, Croydon, CR0 4YY

A CIP record for this book
is available from the British Library

ISBN 978-0-571-38019-0

MIX
Paper | Supporting
responsible forestry
FSC® C171272

Printed and bound in the UK on FSC® certified paper·in line with our continuing
commitment to ethical business practices, sustainability and the environment.

For further information see faber.co.uk/environmental-policy

2 4 6 8 10 9 7 5 3 1

This story is inspired by the whopper
kererū that flew past my office on a
Tuesday morning in May while I was the
University of Otago College of Education
Creative New Zealand Children's
Writer in Residence in 2022 – SH

For Nella – SD

1
The Cat Meaner than Mean Cat

'Does Mean Cat seem a bit different to you?' Dave asked, as he peered out of our shed window.

Dave had wiped clear a spyhole through the thick dirty smear across the middle of the glass. It had been growing more and more grimy since we moved into the shed at the bottom of the Human Lady's garden.

Dave insisted on eating scavenged snacks at the window every evening and now it was splattered in a technicolour mess of crumbs, curry stains and sticky rice bits.

'What do you mean?' I said.

'Does she seem a bit meaner?' he said. 'And maybe a bit stripier?'

Stripier?

I clambered out of the shredded paper nest I'd made by the paint tins and flapped up to join Dave by the window. I expected to see the familiar fluffy cat who had tormented us for four books, who had ripped up Dave's wing and who constantly tried to sabotage our plans to move into her Human Lady's house.

But there, glaring at us from the cat flap

on the opposite side of the garden, was a completely different cat.

'Dave,' I said. 'That's not Mean Cat!'

'I know,' he replied. 'She's changed so much, it's like she's a completely different cat.'

'No!' I insisted. 'That *is* a completely different cat.'

Dave squinted and pressed his beak up against the window. 'Are you sure, Skipper?'

I looked at the menacing face across the garden again. Mean Cat had always had a mean vibe about her but this cat was unlike any cat I'd seen before. She sent a shudder ruffling down the feathers on my back and in that moment it felt like the shed grew darker, as though a storm was coming in overhead. I had to shut my eyes quickly as I felt the cat's stare burn right through me. This cat had a vibe that was meaner than mean.

When I opened my eyes again, I resisted looking back at the menacing face in the cat flap and instead scanned the rest of the garden. I nudged Dave's head down so that he was now looking at the bin because something had caught my eye.

'Yes, I'm sure,' I replied. 'Because if that is Mean Cat, then who is sitting by the bin?'

Dave's eyes widened as he spotted the *actual* Mean Cat by the steel bin. And then he came to the only logical explanation Dave could.

'Mean Cat cloned herself?' he gasped.

I didn't even have to ask how that would've been possible.

'She obviously built herself a science lab and got herself a pair of science goggles for her cat face and a cat-shaped lab coat and then probably made some sort of evil cat laugh-meow sound that would send chills through the actual evil scientists' network,' Dave continued, barely taking a breath. 'She was probably assisted by a moss-covered rock with googly eyes called Steven Melonchunks who, though small, was the actual brains behind the cloning because a cat brain is incapable of making any clever decisions.'

A rock called Steven Melonchunks?

Yes, Skipper. Every bonkers scientist needs a more bonkerser scientist sidekick.

Dave puffed out his chest with an all-knowing authority. 'And then Mean Cat jumped into a bird bath full of baked beans to copy her cat essence.'

Baked beans?

It's the closest thing to what is inside a cat. Keep up, Skipper.

'The cat essence was split in two so she could still stay as Mean Cat but also double up as a *new* Mean Cat . . .'

'That's Aunty's Cat, you fool,' came the voice of Tinkles, the annoying canary who lived with Him-Next-Door.

The golden-yellow fluffball fluttered in through the hole in a wooden panel of the shed door and perched on a nearby shelf.

'Who's Aunty's Cat?' Dave asked, suspiciously.

Tinkles smirked like she was sitting on a treasure map that led to a chest full of jammy biscuits – my favourites.

'If you want to know, it's going to cost you.' Tinkles grinned.

Dave blew out hard from his beak, leaving a smoggy stain on the only clean part of the window.

'What do you want, Tinkles?'

Tinkles strolled along the shelf, lightly dragging the edge of her bright wing along the jars.

'The Human Man has me on a diet of birdseed and air,' she whined. 'It's top quality stuff but it tastes like a baboon's bottom.'

'What's that got to do with us?' I asked.

'I need some of your biscuits to wash the flavour out of my mouth.' Tinkles shrugged.

'And then I'll tell you *everything* you need to know about Aunty's Cat.'

Dave scoffed. 'No. Absolutely not. There's barely enough biscuits for me.'

'Or me,' I chimed in.

We'd been scammed by Tinkles in the past and Dave had barely gotten over the time she invited every single bird in the neighbourhood round to eat all the biscuits in the Human Lady's house.

'Fine,' Tinkles said. She plumped up her feathers and made to look like she was heading off. 'I don't suppose you need to know why even Mean Cat is terrified of her.'

I glanced out of the window again and was struck that Mean Cat didn't seem to be outside for one of her pigeon-ambush patrols, but that instead she was *indeed* cowering behind the bin, hopping from paw to paw, trying to stay out of Aunty's Cat's view.

I never wanted to listen to Tinkles normally. She was full of hot air and canary dust but there was a tense knot in the pit of my belly about Aunty's Cat – I knew I had to go against all my pigeon instincts to find out who exactly this cat was.

'Wait!' I squawked, as Tinkles set off.

She hovered in mid-air. 'Yes?'

'Maybe I have a spare biscuit or two,' I said.

'What are you doing, Skipper?' Dave hissed.

I nudged Dave back to the window. 'Look at Mean Cat. Something isn't right.'

I fished out two jammy biscuits from behind the toolbox and kicked them over to Tinkles. She leapt on them like a hen on eggs.

'This better not be another one of your scams,' I warned Tinkles.

'Oh no,' she said, her beak already full of shortbread and sticky strawberry jam. 'This is the truth about Aunty's Cat and why you should both be scared for your lives.'

2
The Truth About Aunty's Cat

'Long ago, deep beneath the earth, a darkness spread. It took hold like a fire, tornadoing up from the core, erupting in a poisonous gas, choking, stifling—'

'What does this have to do with Aunty's Cat?' I asked Tinkles.

'Nothing,' she said, annoyed by my interruption. 'I just like to start all stories like that.'

'It's true,' Dave said. 'Yesterday Tinkles told me a story about the time she found an old banana skin hanging between the slats of a park bench, and it started exactly the same way.'

Gah! This was not worth giving up two jammy biscuits for. And my grumbling tummy agreed.

'Get to the bit about the alien birds swarming in through the blood-red skies,' Dave egged Tinkles on.

'Dave,' I exclaimed. 'Don't you want to know about Aunty's Cat? Tinkles literally said ten seconds ago that we should be scared for our lives.'

Dave tapped his head with his wing thoughtfully. I knew he was really

struggling. He wanted
to hear the dramatic,
irrelevant story but
also didn't want to lose his
only remaining wing in the
second chapter of our *own* story.

'Dave!' I insisted.

'Fine. Let's hear about Aunty's Cat,' Dave said reluctantly.

Tinkles sighed and plonked herself down like a squashed yellow pom-pom before starting the story of Aunty's Cat.

According to Tinkles, Aunty's Cat belonged to the Human Lady's aunty. Every year the Human Lady's aunty would laden herself with a huge rucksack bursting at the seams, an entire kitchen hanging loose from the straps, and join a group of other Human Aunties. The flock would set off towards the hills in the east for a few days of living outdoors, even though they had perfectly good brick nests to live in normally.

The Human Lady's aunty's cat was never included in this trip because cats are not good at camping. (Or anything really.)

Instead, every time the aunty filled up her bag with toilet roll and tea bags and all the things a Human thinks they need to live outdoors for three days, a car would pull up outside the Human Lady's house and a crate would be dropped off on the doorstep.

And inside the crate would be the very
annoyed and very angry Aunty's Cat.

The only thing you need
to live outdoors is a
TV and a large pizza.

How is a TV
helpful
outdoors?

It's something to
leave your pizza box on
when you are eating
your pizza. Plus it's
great for watching
nature documentaries.

At first glance, the stripy cat with four matching white paws looked like a harmless fuzzball who had slipped her winter socks on.

The very first time Aunty's Cat had visited the Human Lady, Mean Cat had been just a tiny, baby cat, a furry, kitten-brained nuisance of a thing who couldn't tell her left paws from her right paws.

But Aunty's Cat wasn't the sort of cat that was amused by small, furry, kitten-brained nuisances. And while Mean Cat grew more and more attached to the meaner cat, Aunty's Cat made it her life's work to destroy the little kitten.

When Mean Cat tried to share her toys, Aunty's Cat chewed them up and pooped them out. When Mean Cat tried to nap alongside her, Aunty's Cat would open the patio door, kick the little kitten out and lock it. Legend says that Aunty's Cat learned to sharpen her claws into the shape of keys specifically so she could lock Mean Cat out of every room in the house.

For you see, Aunty's Cat had been rescued from a landfill when she herself was a kitten. Oh, and she had been *furious* about it.

The Human Lady's aunty had cherished the fragile kitten from the moment she'd laid eyes on her. The Human had put down her protest sign about the growing landfill and, though it was a cold winter morning, she had taken off her woolly hat and placed

the little kitten gently inside, hugging her close to keep her warm.

And Aunty's Cat was fuming about it. She hated woolly hats. But she hated kindness even more. The angry little kitten's nostrils flared with rage the whole bike ride back to the town.

The kind aunty had taken the kitten home and made her house a sanctuary for the abandoned little beast. She switched out all the food in the house for organic cat nibbles and she replaced all the furniture with deeply scratchable alternatives. Rumour had it that she even changed her antique staircase for a highly complicated cat scratching post, making it almost impossible for Humans to get upstairs to the bathroom. But she didn't mind. She wanted this lost little kitten to feel completely and utterly loved.

This gesture of unconditional love enraged Aunty's Cat ferociously.

It didn't make much sense, and

birds have tried for years and years to understand why this cat was so angry. The only sensible conclusion was ...

Baked beans. I knew it was baked beans all along.

... that it had nothing to do with baked beans and everything to do with a fear of being abandoned again.

The more that the cat was loved, the more afraid the cat became of losing all the love she'd gained. So she hardened up. She sharpened those nails and perfected her snarl. And she decided to be the meanest cat the world had ever seen.

Tinkles dropped her head. 'We have lost hundreds of birds to that cat,' she said.

Tinkles listed the names of the fallen. She told us about Parakeet Parker who had only just escaped from a zoo when he was caught by Aunty's Cat.

'We only knew him as Paratha Parker after that.' Tinkles sighed as she remembered the feast Aunty's Cat had made of him.

Tinkles went on and I found myself unable to concentrate. My wings felt clammy and when I looked down, I saw my claws had turned white from gripping the ledge with fear.

Dave looked over at me wide-eyed. 'I don't want to be one of the hundreds,' he exclaimed, panicking as Tinkles carried on with the long roll call of names.

I caught a glimpse of myself in the side of a silver tin of paint. My face looked just like Dave's.

I didn't want to be one of the hundreds either.

3

This May Be the End of This Story Because WE'RE GOING TO DIE

I nearly jumped fully out of my feathers at the sound of two cats hissing and spitting at each other in the garden. And then—

BAM!

The two beasts smashed into each other,

crashing into the bin. Bin bags and plastic bottles went flying into the air as the cats battled amongst rotten vegetable skins and old yoghurt pots on the grass. Tinkles shot out of the shed the way she came in, darting over the fence back to her home.

'Was that me?' Dave screeched. 'Have I exploded?'

'No! It's Aunty's Cat.' I was panicking. 'She's floored Mean Cat!'

'We're going to die!' Dave cried.

We didn't even have time to dart for the window. The door sprang open and a stripy monstrosity leapt at us.

Aunty's Cat!

I took off, soaring into the rafters as Dave ran for the hedge trimmer. The beast hurdled the motor of the strimmer, trapping Dave in the corner of the shed.

'SKIPPER!' Dave screamed at the top of his feathers.

I dived for the corner, ready to peck at the vicious monster's head. I snapped in my wings close to my sides, getting faster and faster as the cat licked her sharp teeth and sneered at Dave.

But just as I swooped in to save Dave, Aunty's Cat whipped her head back and opened her jaws wide. I misjudged my landing and plunged straight into her mouth.

'NOOOOOO!' I screamed.

I kicked out my legs, pushing her teeth apart, stretching and stretching so she couldn't clamp her jagged jaws around me.

Dave staggered towards her with an armful of paint sponges, lobbing them, one after the other, into her huge, gaping mouth.

'WHAT ARE YOU DOING?' I screeched, not sure if I could keep stretching any more.

'Giving you a softer landing,' Dave yelled back.

Before I could scream at him for being the worst best friend in history, the sponges did something magical. Aunty's Cat heaved. She coughed. She heaved again. The sponges were drying out the old cat's throat.

'Sponge her again!' I shouted at Dave.

He threw in the last of the sponges and she hacked me up like a hairball, sending me cartwheeling towards Dave.

We didn't have a second to hang around. We raced for the open door and into the garden towards the Human Lady's house.

The coughing monster dashed after us. She was on Dave's tail within moments, tearing at his feathers like a furry evil lawnmower.

I spotted an opening under the house where the trellis had broken away leaving a route into a crawl space.

'Come on, Dave,' I screamed at my friend.

'HELP,' Dave screeched back. 'She's

almost got me!'

'We'll be safe in here!' I shrieked, turning back and dragging Dave the last ten beaks into the opening under the house.

Safe in the space, we could hear Aunty's Cat scratching and screeching in the garden, livid that she hadn't finished us off. She was too big to scramble in under the house.

'Thank feathers for the holes in the Human Lady's nest,' Dave breathed. 'That was close.'

I collapsed next to him, trying to catch my breath, but my voice caught in my beak at the thought of what could have been.

We were almost pigeon soup.

'I'm glad I found us this excellent hiding spot,' Dave said smugly.

I glowered at him – he'd mostly been screaming about being too pretty to die and generally being useless the whole time.

'If I hadn't said "We're going to die",' he continued, tapping his head. 'I was the inspiration. It's called forward thinking, Skipper.'

Dave, you never think ahead. If anything, you usually completely forget to think. I have to do most of the thinking for both of us.

It was dark under the house and it was taking my eyes a while to adjust. I could just about make out the shape of Dave pottering around as he tried to work out where we were. Or at least if there was any food under here with us.

A sound caught my earholes. It was a tinkly drip and I knew immediately it was coming from the crack in the drainpipe where Dave had once tried to smash an old loaf into breadcrumbs. Only we'd mistaken an old loaf for a brick. And all Dave had done was damage a pipe that seemed important to the Human Lady's nest.

Water had slowly started to seep out of the crack over the following weeks and now there was a constant gentle drip that flowed straight from the Human Lady's bath drain down to the bottom of the house. It created a refreshing grey swimming pool for me and Dave to lounge in on hot summer days.

I followed the sound and washed the

slimy cat spit from my body, feeling better
with each shake of my feathers.

'Hey, look, Skipper!' Dave shouted at me
in the dark. 'I found a really cosy corner.'

I followed his squawk to the other corner
of the crawl space and in the dim light I
could make out my friend fluffing a furry
cushion.

'Look how comfy this blanket is,' Dave
said, wrapping a long end of the fur over
his belly and snuggling into the pelts of
softness.

I peered closer. There was something
awfully familiar about the blanket.

The sleek fur rippled in the shadows and
when I got close, a warmth radiated from
the fleecy coating.

And that's when I caught a sharp whiff of wee and grass.

'Dave,' I whispered, my voice trembling. 'That's not a blanket. That's a tail!'

4
The Purring Blanket

The blanket swelled, rocking Dave off his bottom and on to his belly.

There was no mistaking the all too recognisable stench of cat. And the growl that we had been avoiding for years.

It was Mean Cat.

I gulped. Only Dave would try and wrap himself in our arch enemy's tail and land us right in the jaws of death.

'Don't make any sudden movements,' I

murmured out of the side of my beak to Dave.

He was still on his belly, frozen in fear.

'Heeeeeelp,' he whispered back, his voice breaking.

I edged towards Dave, carefully raising a claw and then gently placing it back on the ground without making a sound, all the while never taking my eyes off the grizzling cat. When I felt my friend's quivering feathers by my side, I eased down slowly. I nudged Dave over with my foot, rolling him on to his back, and then we both shuffled slowly towards the opposite corner, me taking it one pigeon step at a time and him one pigeon bottom shuffle by one pigeon bottom shuffle.

We made it all the way to the back corner and as far from Mean Cat as possible in the dark hole. Mean Cat stayed where she was, groaning and meowing. I was extremely grateful to have all my feathers but a thought jumped into my head that I just couldn't shake out: *why wasn't she coming after us?*

This was the best opportunity she'd ever had to finish us off for good. In all the time we had known her, she'd wanted to chomp us down like a couple of pigeon burgers with a side of fresh feather fries, but now she didn't seem to care we were there.

Had she even noticed us? Maybe she'd

lost her sense of smell and sight and general cat-ness, and she had no idea Dave had just tried to wear her like a jacket.

I stayed quiet, not willing to risk that she might see us eventually. But Dave's idea of quiet was inching himself back on his bum and whispering the word 'heeeeeelp' – except his whispers were as loud as an aeroplane engine.

'Something isn't right,' I said quietly to Dave.

'What do you mean, Skipper?' Dave panicked. 'You know I don't mean to make those smells. It only happens when I'm scared.'

'Not that,' I flapped. '*Her*,' I said, pointing a wing into the dimly lit space in front of us.

Now that our eyes had adjusted to the dark, I could make out Mean Cat completely.

She was pacing the small space, meowing uncomfortably, her eyes darting around like she was waiting for something.

Dave stood up and brushed down his feathers. He cocked his head and looked at our long-time nemesis.

'You're right,' Dave declared. 'She hasn't come after me once.'

He puffed out his chest, all annoyed and huffy.

'What's wrong with me?' he went on, clearly peeved by Mean Cat's snub. He looked down at his belly and patted the jelly-shaped dome with his good wing. 'I'm still a fabulously tasty morsel.'

He got to his feet and stalked right over to Mean Cat, who was now so disinterested in my friend she barely gave him a glance, and instead had a good old lick of her underbelly.

'Excuse me, Mean Cat,' Dave said. 'Am I not tasty enough for you?'

My eyes almost popped out of my head in shock. 'What are you doing?!' I squawked at my friend.

'Plenty of other cats would want a piece of me,' Dave continued. 'I'm premium pigeon, you know. Completely organic.'

I wasn't entirely sure about that. Dave had eaten and completely digested a plastic library card yesterday, but at that moment I didn't have time to argue with him about what an 'organic' pigeon was. He was about to turn us both into dinnertime.

That library card was completely organic. It was fresh out of the plastic-laminating machine.

That's not what organic means, Dave. Organic stuff comes from fresh, living things.

That laminator was definitely alive. It almost laminated my head!

I vaulted at my friend, tackling him to the ground and clasping a wing over his beak before he could say anything more.

'She's going to eat us both if you aren't careful,' I hissed at him.

We tussled on the floor, Dave trying to break free and me trying to keep him quiet. As we rolled in the dark, there was a high-pitched whine which stopped us mid-wrestle.

'What was that?' Dave gulped.

And then we were showered in what felt like gooey sewer juice. It clung to every inch of our feathers, gluing us to each other.

'Skipper, I don't think she's going to eat anyone anytime soon,' Dave spluttered, spitting the liquid from his beak. 'She's just been sick on us.'

I spun around, ripping myself away from Dave before we were stuck fast. There was a pool of goo around Mean Cat. Only it was the wrong end of her to be a pool of sick.

I wiped the gloop from my eyes with my wing and blew out the globules clogging my beak.

Once I'd shaken most of it out of my feathers, I examined the puddle around Mean Cat, kicking it with my claw and dripping it back on to the ground.

'Careful, Skipper!' Dave yelped. 'There's something in there.'

He was right.

The gloop moved and wriggled. It

writhed and stirred and every time the dim light in the dark space hit it, it gleamed and squirmed some more, like there was something buried deep inside the thick liquid.

I took a step closer, feeling Dave's breath on my back as he shielded behind me.

'Is that . . .' he stammered. 'Is that what I think it is?'

My mouth fell open.

'I think it is,' I murmured back.

'Oh, pigeon squeakers!' Dave cried, gripping me to stop himself from collapsing in shock. 'It's finally happening! We are being invaded by alien cats!'

I looked my friend straight in the eye. 'Dave, those aren't aliens!' I laughed. I couldn't help the smile spreading across my beak. 'Those are newborn kittens!'

Same thing.

5

Mama Dave

'Mean Cat made *more* mean cats,' I exclaimed.

Mean Cat gently licked her babies clean one by one as they emerged from the gloop.

Dave let out a coo and I knew immediately that his insides had melted like warm chocolate. He made the same sound when he saw baby chicks at the petting zoo.

He counted out the kittens. One, two, three, four. All carbon copies of Mean Cat but tinier, with four delicate little paws a piece. All but one. The fourth was grey from her mini nose to the tips of her back paws. She seemed to sense me in the dark, and her little face turned towards me even though her eyelids were shut tight.

'Skipper, I'm not sure they are *mean* cats,' Dave said, unable to stop the gushing in his voice as he gazed upon the babies, all wobbly on their newborn paws.

'Dave, no,' I said abruptly.

'What do you mean "no"?' he asked, turning to me.

'You are doing that thing you do when you get all gooey-eyed,' I warned. 'This is an army of mean cats and they are going to *destroy* us.'

'Or maybe they are just adorable little

bubbakins,' he said, babbling at the little grey one who was stumbling on her paws.

'They are lions,' I cried. 'Baby, vicious LIONS!'

Two of the kittens bumped heads and tumbled on to their bottoms, then one rolled on his back like an upside-down turtle.

'*Or*,' Dave started, 'maybe they are just innocent babies.' He tentatively took a step towards the kittens. 'Normal, innocent babies. And *maybe* if they get used to us, we can *train* them not to eat pigeons.'

I eyed Dave suspiciously. 'Train them?'

'Yup,' Dave replied. 'Just like you can train a rhino.'

Dave hugged me like a proud uncle. 'Look how cute they are!'

I had to admit there was something inside me thawing too. Perhaps it was their mini paws with the tiniest of boopable pads on the undersides. Or perhaps it was the way Dave was tenderly gazing upon the little bubs. But I couldn't help but feel a bit protective towards the cute little newborns.

And then I remembered Mean Cat. I shot a glance at her and spotted her giving me and Dave a hard stare. I'd seen this look before. We had between five and eight seconds to get out of there or we were going to be minced pigeon.

I braced myself to make a run for the back wall.

But then she did something I'd never seen her do before. She gave us a small nod, before lying her head down on the concrete floor and shutting her eyes.

'Is she dead?' Dave whispered.

'No,' I replied. 'I think she's resting.' I counted out the babies again. 'It must be quite tiring giving birth to four kittens.'

'I know exactly how she feels. I'm completely knackered after a big poop,' Dave nodded.

'I don't think that's the same, Dave.'

'I'm not talking a regular poo. I'm talking one of the ones you have after eating a large pizza all by yourself. It's always easily the size of four mini mean cats,' Dave insisted.

The kittens purred contentedly, now nuzzling Mean Cat and having their first milk.

Next to me I could hear Dave salivating.

'Don't even think about it, Dave.'

'I would never drink from the enemy,' he said but he seemed disappointed at not having a milkshake right at that very moment.

Mean Cat sighed. Her breath heavy and exhausted.

Once Mean Cat was snoring, Dave began to fuss over the kittens again.

'Can we keep them?' he asked me.

'No!' I exclaimed. 'After everything Mean Cat's done to us, you want to keep the mini Mean Cats?' I pointed at his torn wing to remind him what mean cats did.

'But she's fast asleep and they need us,' he insisted. 'Remember when my brother was just a little eggling?'

'Yes?'

'And remember how he kept falling out of the nest?'

I giggled. 'He fell out four times and landed on his head.'

'If we look after the babies, we can stop them falling out of the nest,' Dave said. 'We can protect them.'

'Dave, we're on the floor. They're not falling anywhere.'

Dave flapped me quiet as the little grey kitten coaxed its way over a couple of the others towards us. The plumpness of my feathered friend seemed to make the kittens sleepy, and they burrowed around our feet, settling against Dave like he was a beanbag chair.

'I suppose they *are* quite cute,' I said reluctantly, now encircled by little kittens. 'And they are extremely soft,' I added, giving Dave a small smile.

As I shuffled on my bottom to get comfy, the kittens snuggled in closer, yawning with their teeny-tiny mouths. With the ring of kittens around us both, I was overwhelmed by a feeling of peace, like eating sweet strawberries on a summer's day.

'You should tell them a story, Skipper,' Dave said excitedly. 'Babies like stories.'

He petted the grey one with his wing. 'Tell them the story about a swashbuckling pigeon who had four knives and a crew of wobbly eggs.'

'Good idea!' I chuckled.

He wrapped his good wing around the grey kitten who had now taken quite a liking to Dave. When he thought I wasn't looking, I saw him give the kitten the tenderest of pecks on her head.

'Hey, Skipper, this little grey one looks a bit like me, don't you think?' Dave grinned. He peered down at the kitten so they were beak to nose. 'I think I'm going to name her Dave Too.'

6
Kitten Rescue!

MAAARRRAO!!

'What was that?' I yelped.

CRASH!

There was another yowl of MAARRRRAO followed by an implosion of splinters from the trellis wall as it was smashed into.

Aunty's Cat was trying to break in!

'The kittens!' I screamed at Dave.

You know if you hear the cat screech and count the seconds between that and the crash, that will tell you how far away Aunty's Cat is.

Dave, I think you're confusing that with thunder. If you see the lightning and count the seconds before you hear the thunder, that tells you how far away it is.

Works for cats too. And confused camels. And ice-cream vans.

The criss-crossed barricade between us and the beast heaved under the pressure of Aunty's Cat's attack. Her nose was pressed up hard against the gaps in the trellis as she clawed and tore at the disintegrating wood, snarling at us as she spotted the kittens.

'We must save Dave Too at all costs,' Dave cried, hugging tight the kitten who looked nothing like him. They weren't even the same grey.

Mean Cat lay on her side, exhausted, as the little kittens continued to nuzzle her underbelly for snacks. The noise woke her and she raised her head and caught my eye. I saw something I'd never seen before in the cat – there was a dark, haunted look in her eyes and she started to tremble with fear as it dawned on her that there were now just five splinters of wood keeping her and her babies safe from Aunty's Cat.

'We need to protect Dave Three, Dave Dave and Davey-Diddly-Doo-Dave too!' Dave yelled.

'You named them all?' I yelled back.

'They needed names. We couldn't keep calling them "the kittens" – they are all individuals!'

'But you named them all Dave.'

'It's a solid name,' Dave replied.

'You didn't name a single one after me?'

'None of them look like you, Skipper.'

'None of them look like you, Dave! You're a pigeon!'

A yowl from behind stopped us mid-argument.

'It's Mean Cat,' Dave panicked. He grabbed on to me, his body a quivering jelly of feathers. 'We're finished!'

Mean Cat craned her neck higher and stared over at the trellis which now had a huge crack down the middle from the strain of Aunty's Cat's slashing. Mean Cat's eyes grew wide like two saucers of milk.

She leapt to her feet and shoved the babies behind her fluffy body. She grabbed the back of my head and threw me towards the kittens.

'What do you want from me?' Dave pleaded with the cat. 'I'm not ready to die!'

She kicked him aside and looked me dead in the eye before nodding to the opposite corner of the crawl space as Aunty's Cat made the final break through the trellis.

Mean Cat pounced on Aunty's Cat, her claws drawn like weapons. They snarled and hissed at each other as paws flew like cannonballs across a sea of cat fur. Aunty's Cat snatched Mean Cat up in her jaws and hurled her to the ground, raining arrows of claws into the weaker animal.

'We have to get the babies out of here,' I screamed at Dave over the two shrieking cats.

With the trellis down, light burst into the dark space and I could see now that there was a large mouse hole in the opposite corner. I knew this mouse hole! It was the one that led to the Human Lady's living room. *That's* where Mean Cat wanted us to go. That's how we could *save* the kittens.

'In there!' I screamed, shoving Dave and Dave Too towards the hole.

Dave scooped up Dave Too and rolled towards the opposite corner. He clambered up through the hole with Dave Too wrapped in his good wing, propelling himself with all his might to safety.

But within seconds, I heard a distressed squawk.

'I'm stuck, Skipper,' he yelled.

His legs dangled free but his bottom was wedged in the hole.

'Suck in your bum,' I screamed.

'It *is* sucked in!' he screeched back.

The warring cats were now clawing at each other and inching closer by the second towards my trapped friend.

I grabbed Dave Three, Dave Dave and Davey-Diddly-Doo-Dave and charged at Dave's feathery bum. Headbutting him with all my might, I squeezed us all into the hole and hurled the rest of the kittens through to safety.

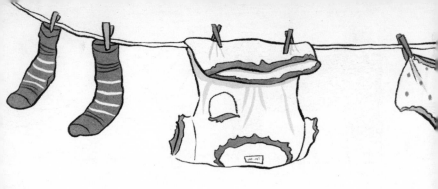

7

All Kittens Grow Up to Be Mean Cats. Dave Too, Too.

Up in the house we couldn't hear the cats battling outside. Maybe Aunty's Cat had finally defeated Mean Cat and was wearing her as a fur coat.

We rolled the unsteady kittens on to the rug in the warm living room.

The house was full of its familiar smells of baking bread and just-dried laundry.

I squawked loudly to let the Human Lady know we were there. But the house was silent, so it was up to me and Dave to look after the little fuzzballs.

Dave set up camp with Dave Too in one of the Human Lady's fluffy slippers and I took the other three over to Mean Cat's blanket. The cat stench coming off the luxury plush throw seemed to calm the babies and they nestled together, falling into a comfortable sleep. This gave me time to work out a plan with Dave.

'We don't know how to look after baby cats,' I panicked, completely in over my beak thanks to another one of Dave's cat-brained ideas. How I had been convinced to look after a bunch of kittens when we could have escaped to safety four chapters ago I do not know, but Dave had done it again. 'They need their mean-cat mum, not a couple of pigeons who know nothing about kittens,' I told Dave.

'I'm not going out there to get her,' Dave scoffed. 'Did you see what Aunty's Cat was doing to Mean Cat? We wouldn't stand a chance.'

I gazed at the little ones. 'But their mum—' I started.

'But me,' Dave finished. 'I'd be torn in half if I went back there, and Dave Too needs *me*.'

He folded himself around the shivering little grey kitten who soon warmed up against my friend's snuggly feathers.

'What do baby cats even eat?' I whispered, as the bundled kittens on the blanket started to gently snore in unison. 'They'll be awake soon and looking for food.'

'My guess is pizza,' Dave suggested.

'Pizza?'

'That's what I would eat if I was a baby,' he said, all matter-of-fact. 'With a stuffed crust and everything.'

Mine and Dave's thoughts of a baby's first food were interrupted by a tap at the window.

It was Tinkles.

'Stay very still, Skipper,' Dave mumbled out the side of his beak. 'She may not notice us.'

'Yoo-hoo, boys,' Tinkles sang from the other side of the window where she could very much see us. 'Could you open the latch for us?'

Us?

I dragged my wings over to the window, jumping on to the ledge, and flipped up the metal lock with my beak. The window sprang open and Tinkles hopped in, followed by a posse of five other birds.

'Hey, it's Fountain Pete,' I called down to Dave.

He'd brought along the rest of the park pigeon crew. There was Little Sev, who was in fact the biggest of the lot, Little Little Sev, who was a bit smaller than Little Sev but not quite the smallest of the group, Quiffo Pavu, who always had something to say and a generous quiff to whip, and Noisy Boi, who nobody had ever heard say anything ever.

'We just thought we'd come and congratulate you on your new brood,' Quiffo Pavu said. He whipped his quiff and nodded at me and Dave. 'Tinkles told us as soon as she heard the two cats in that showdown outside.'

'We were a bit surprised to hear *you two*

had rescued the kittens,' Little Little Sev said. There was something in his voice that told me he was not too pleased about that.

'We couldn't really leave them there,' I said, sensing the growing tension from the park pigeons. 'They're just babies. Who knows what Aunty's Cat might have done?'

'Absolutely!' Pavu piped up. 'Just innocents.'

He hopped down to join Dave in the slipper and eyed up Dave Too. 'Just innocent creatures. A bit like us birds, don't you think?'

Dave's eyes narrowed. 'What are you suggesting?'

'Well, my friend,' Pavu went on, flipping his quiff. 'They start off innocent and then they grow up to be cats. Cats who grow up to attack *actual* innocents like us.'

My mouth dried. 'What are you suggesting?'

'I'm suggesting you do the right thing,' Pavu said. 'Be a pal. Let them loose. If they survive, well, good on 'em, but if they don't, that's one less future mean cat to be worried about.'

Dave gasped, pulling Dave Too close to his chest and covering her ears. 'These little things wouldn't last a minute out there and you know it.'

Fountain Pete stepped in. 'And neither would we, now there's four little ones who'll grow up in no time to be four big ones with a taste for pigeon.'

'Even Mean Cat started off like those kittens once,' Little Sev said, joining Pavu and Fountain Pete. 'But she still became a pigeon-attacking beast, didn't she?'

We all stared at Dave's broken wing.

They weren't wrong. As much as Dave believed Mean Cat was dropped – a full-sized, fully formed cat – from the sky in an alien cat attack gone wrong, the truth was I was eighty-five per cent sure she was probably just born a regular kitten like the little ones she herself had birthed earlier.

The smile I'd had on my beak since we saved the babies started to waver. My gaze ping-ponged from Dave's broken wing to the little kitten squabs fast asleep in their peaceful huddle.

There was a tightness in my chest that was starting to grow as I realised the park pigeons were right. I expected Dave to be feeling the same but when I looked up at him, he was standing tall with his chest puffed out. He flashed me a reassuring smile and hugged Dave Too close again.

'I have a plan,' Dave announced.

Oh no. Not a Dave plan.

'What if we turn them into pigeons?' he suggested.

8
Kitten Pigeons

'Are you off your eggs?' Fountain Pete mocked. His face contorted into an expression of horror, like he'd just seen a pigeon in Human clothes.

'No!' Dave insisted. 'What *if* we teach them to be pigeons? We'd have our own little army on the inside, ready to defend us against their *own* kind?'

'Cats is cats and pigeons is pigeons,' Noisy Boi said.

There was absolute silence in the room as we all turned to stare at Noisy Boi. Nobody had ever heard him speak before.

'You're Scottish?' Dave gasped.

Pavu cleared his beak. 'Dave, you are missing the point,' he said. 'There is no way to change an animal's destiny.'

Pavu was right. In all of nature, the one thing that was for sure was an animal's destiny. Lions were destined to rule the Serengetti, just as pigeons were destined to rule fountains, and bookworms were destined to rule libraries.

Training the kittens to be pigeons wasn't actually Dave's worst idea and as I watched him pet Dave Too, I could see he had formed a bond with the little cat that he wasn't ready to break. But his idea was sadly the one that was the most unlikely to succeed. Cats were indeed cats and pigeons were very much pigeons.

'Just give the kittens a chance!' Dave pleaded.

Pavu glanced up at the clock on the wall. (I don't know why. Pigeons have no idea what those ticking wall circles are for.) 'You can try all you like.' He shrugged. 'But we can't help. And we won't help.'

The Sevs, Fountain Pete and Noisy Boi all nodded in agreement. Even Tinkles joined in.

'I was destined to live a life of fancy bird food and filtered water and you two were destined to live in a shed fighting over stale biscuit crumbs,' she sang.

'We don't fight over stale biscuit crumbs,' Dave argued with Tinkles.

It was true. Dave usually only got

into an argument with me if it was stale breadcrumbs.

'Look,' Pavu interrupted Dave. 'The ice-cream van is due at the park soon and someone needs to crack open that box of wafer cones before the Human Kids arrive after school.'

He shot a final glance at the kittens and then shook his head sadly.

'You know what *we* would do if it was us,' Fountain Pete said, as he nodded to the babies who were starting to stir in their sleep.

The pigeons headed back towards the open window, taking Tinkles with them.

'Turn them into pigeons?' I cried at Dave as soon as they'd left.

'You're welcome.' Dave beamed at me. 'What would you do without me?'

'We can't turn kittens into pigeons,' I exclaimed. 'Sometimes we can barely convince pigeons they're pigeons!'

Dave grimaced. 'Oh. I forgot about the time that cousin of yours genuinely thought he could live in a freshwater fish tank.'

'Why would anyone even want to be a pigeon?' I sulked. 'You heard what Tinkles said about us.'

Dave left Dave Too to sleep in the fluffy slipper and came over to sit next to me. He put his good wing out and pulled me in for a hug.

'You can't listen to Tinkles,' Dave said.

'She's barely a bird. She looks like the inside of a cooked egg.'

We both shuddered at the idea of an egg being cooked.

'Don't let her get in your head,' Dave said. 'Being a pigeon is the best thing anyone could ever wish to be.'

'Right,' I mocked. 'Because everyone wants to scrap for food down at the bins, don't they? And everyone wants to sleep in the cold each night. Oh, and let's not forget that *everyone* wants to spend their days being chased by cats, dogs who have mistaken

pigeons for squirrels, small children, balloons, buses, annoyed Humans with umbrellas, annoyed Humans with walking sticks, annoyed Humans with baguettes—'

'You know what I hear when you list those things?' Dave said, stopping me mid-sentence. 'I hear the excitement of not knowing where you are going to dine each day, the adventure of sleeping in the great outdoors and being the most popular resident in the neighbourhood, so much so that everyone wants to spend time with you.'

My beak fell open. 'You got that from what I just said?'

'Yes, Skipper.' Dave grinned. 'Being a pigeon is the best. And if I was a kitten, I would want to grow up to be a pigeon.'

The baby cats started to stir again on the blanket and I gazed down at them. They were all helpless and alone. We were all they had.

Maybe Dave was right. Maybe being a pigeon wasn't as terrible as Tinkles made it out to be. And if Dave was right about this, maybe, just maybe, he was right about changing the kittens' destinies.

Was it possible to turn these kittens into *pigeons*?

Then I remembered every single cat-brained idea Dave had convinced me to follow since the day I met him, and how many times I had almost been swallowed, nuggeted, out-pirated, trapped in a dungeon and rolled up by a panda, and how many times I had very nearly not made it out alive.

Nope. Dave's idea was as daft as all the rest of them.

MAAARRRRAO!!

Mean Cat smashed through the cat flap in the kitchen and bounded into the living room.

'She's coming for me!' Dave cried.

I grabbed Dave's wing and we clung to each other, barricading the babies from the incoming cat.

Mean Cat launched at us and flung herself over our heads, wrapping up the kittens under her belly.

Mean Cat's rasping breaths felt hot against my feathers. Her body trembled and I could feel the ground under me quake. She was afraid and she stared at me with fear in her eyes, unblinking.

That's when I heard Dave counting so loudly it was like he was in my head.

'Six pigeons,

seven pigeons,

eight pigeons.'

SLAM.

'Aunty's Cat is eight pigeons away, Skipper,' Dave panicked.

SLAM.

Mean Cat must have lodged the cat flap shut so Aunty's Cat was locked out. But the three of us knew it wouldn't be long before she got in and we were all pigeon-kitten marmalade on toast.

I gripped Dave and turned to Mean Cat, giving her a nod that said we would call a truce for a moment to save the kittens.

Mean Cat nodded back.

For one chapter and one chapter only, we were about to team up with Mean Cat to get rid of the meanest cat there had ever been.

9
The Truce

'Mean Cat, cover the door,' I squawked.

She didn't have a clue what I said, being a cat brain and all, but she saw me shoot a desperate glance at the door to the living room and ran for it.

Dave's counting got louder and louder by the second.

'Two pigeons,

three PIGEONS,

FOUR PIGEONS!'

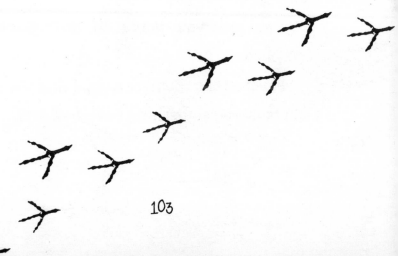

103

SLAM!

'Dave, you need to protect the babies,' I shrieked at my friend.

'What?' He gulped. 'That seems dangerous!'

'Or you can be the bait.'

'Which is why I should do the dangerous job of protecting the babies,' he agreed fast, balling the kittens up on the blanket and sitting on them like he was going to hatch four furry eggs.

I was stuck with the only job left: the bait.

'What are you going to do?' Dave screeched.

I searched the room for a plan. And then I remembered something Pavu had said.

'The ice-cream van!' I shrieked back at Dave.

'This isn't the time to think about wafer cones and sprinkles, Skipper!'

'No, Dave!' I yelled. 'The ice-cream van means it's the library bus day too!'

'What use is a story now?' Dave cried. 'We're all going to be pigeon pakoras in a minute.'

I didn't have time to explain to Dave. We were running out of time and for this plan to work, everything had to be perfectly choreographed.

Every day, when the hands on the clock looked like Dave's granny at a disco, the Human Library Bus drove past the house. The Human Man behind the wheel always had his window rolled down. In the summer, the spring, the winter and even in a tornado once.

If we timed this right, Aunty's Cat would run to the living room, would realise there was pigeon on offer, chase me down, go flying through the unlatched window and straight into the library bus as it passed by. Then she would circle the town twice and be parked up at the library bus depot until next week when hopefully she was so disorientated she would never return to the Human Lady's house again.

But this was all about timing.

We couldn't have a single thing go wrong.

I stared up at the ticking wall circle. The clock hit Disco Time and, right on cue, Aunty's Cat smashed through the cat flap and leapt straight at Mean Cat. They tussled and screeched like two mop heads ensnared in barbed wire.

'Do something,' Dave screamed at me.

I swooped down and yanked Mean Cat off Aunty's Cat, dropping her in a heap on the couch.

Aunty's Cat took the bait and leapt at me.

I dived for the window, it's unsecured latch flapping in the breeze, clanging against the wooden frame.

The library bus was coming and almost in position.

'Come and get me, you cat-brained brute!' I screamed.

Aunty's Cat launched her entire body into the air just as I knocked into the window and nudged it open.

I jumped back through into the house as Anuty's Cat crashed through the open frame and flew towards the library bus.

Then she smashed face first into the very rolled-up, very shut window.

For the first time ever, the bus window was shut.

The library bus rolled on down the road, leaving Aunty's Cat strewn out like a dazed, flattened bathmat on the pavement.

'Is she dead?' Dave whispered, as he pressed his beak up against the window.

Mean Cat pressed up next to us, her smooshed face more smooshed against the glass.

Aunty's Cat wobbled and swayed as she got to her feet just as a Human walked past. He knelt down to stroke her back but Aunty's Cat snarled at him.

'She's not dead,' I said to Dave.

The beastly cat stared at the three of us perched in the window. There was a cold, defeated look in her eyes but she stuck out her chin and gave us a glare that said she'd be back one day to seek revenge.

10
New Homes for the Kittens and Dave Too, Too.

But that day wouldn't happen for a while.

The Human Lady arrived home to find her window flapping wildly in the wind, a note on her doorstep about a squashed cat that had wandered off down the road never to be seen again and four brand-new kittens snuggled up against a very tired Mean Cat.

She tended to Mean Cat, looking after

the new mum by setting up a cat spa that included a small cat massage chair.

The clever Human Lady knew exactly what to feed brand-new kittens and it turned out it was not pizza, which was great because it meant more pizza crusts for us.

She nursed the little ones until they were big enough to stand on their own paws without wibble-wobbling all over the place. Their faces fluffed out and their eyes grew big and it wasn't long before she said the words Dave was dreading: 'We'll have to find new homes for you all.'

Aunty's Cat's Human returned from her trip with her bag full of ridiculous things, and was stunned to find her cat was no longer here. She seemed sad about it, her eyes small and puffy as she cried into the cup of tea the Human Lady made her.

But her downturned shoulders soon straightened up and her trembling chin stilled as little Davey-Diddly-Doo-Dave, who was quite taken by the Human who smelled of fresh air and backpack, made himself at home in her lap. The two bonded over a TV show about snow monkeys with red faces and a love for rocks, and after a few weeks were sent off home together.

(Rumour had it that Aunty's Cat joined a pack of city foxes and became their leader. They moved out of town and set up a commune in the woods where they roamed as a gang, stealing woolly hats from campers and kicking out the pegs that secured the Human tents.)

Fountain Pete came over a few days later to check on Dave's promise to turn the kittens into pigeons. Unfortunately the kittens remained kittens and Pigeon Training Camp was a complete disaster.

'Well, it's not gone to plan,' Dave explained to Fountain Pete. 'Dave Too is our only success story.'

'Dave Three and Dave Dave failed Pigeon Training Camp,' I reported. 'They were too distracted by a shard of light on the shed wall, I'm afraid.' I pointed to the kittens who were still chasing the same spot of light on the wall. 'They've been trying to catch that thing for two days.'

'Cat brains,' Fountain Pete scoffed at the daft kittens.

We'd tried to teach the kittens to perch on ledges just like a pigeon, poop mid-flight and even pick out the best biscuits from an unattended picnic hamper, but it was no use – they all made terrible pigeons.

'I taught Dave Too to fly,' Dave announced just as a disappointed Fountain Pete was about to leave.

'You did?' Fountain Pete and I exclaimed, confused.

'I did,' Dave beamed.

We couldn't take our eyes off Dave and Dave Too as Dave tried to roll, headbutt, belly-nudge and shove Dave Too on top of a paint tin. Eventually the kitten, who refused to budge, trod on Dave and pounced on to the tin, leaving Dave beak-down on the shed floor.

Dave dusted himself off and puffed out his chest. Then he commanded, 'Fly, Dave Too, fly!'

Dave Too licked her paws.

'Come on, Dave Too! You can do it,' Dave encouraged.

Dave Too yawned and instead curled up in a ball on the tin lid.

It was a classic Dave plan going classically the way it always did.

Fountain Pete coughed and cleared his beak. 'She doesn't seem to be doing much flying, Dave.'

'I'm sure she's flying in her mind,' Dave said, cheerfully.

The kittens were cats through and through, and as they got bigger each day, their brains got smaller, just like a cat's.

'We can't keep them,' I said to Dave. 'They will never be pigeons.'

'But Dave Too has so much potential,' Dave replied, giving me his biggest pigeon eyes. 'She reminds me so much of me as a baby.'

What can you possibly remember about being a baby? Nobody remembers being a baby.

No, you don't!

I remember being in my egg.

I do! It smelled of egg and was very eggy.

Dave insisted on keeping up the training with Dave Too and as he continued her Pigeon Training Camp lessons in the garden, it was up to me to keep watch as our truce with Mean Cat had very much finished the second Aunty's Cat strode off down the road. Mean Cat had gone back to her old ways, hissing at us and threatening us with her sharp claws if we dared try to make our way into the Human Lady's house.

Thanks to Dave and his camp, I became an expert at dodging cat attacks from the over-protective mum in the kitchen, in the living room, in the bit between the kitchen and living room and in the bit between the kitchen floor and the living-room ceiling.

You're welcome, Skipper.

Over the next few weeks, the Human Lady carried on caring for the kittens. But within a month she had found homes for all the kittens, including Dave Too.

Dave Three went to the Little Human down the road. He already had a cat of his own, so he knew exactly what to do with another cat-brained cat.

Dave Dave was adopted by an Old Human who Dave and I were very familiar with. She always had sweets in her pockets, which were usually sticky and warm from sitting by the radiator where she hung her coat in the library. Dave had once got trapped in her pocket after his beak got stuck to one of those sweets.

Mmmm, toffee. It was totally worth it.

And then there was Dave Too. Dave struggled with her adoption the most. A kind Human Man who worked with the Human Lady came over to see Dave Too. Dave tried to poop on his head but missed and hit Mean Cat instead. Then when the Human Man attempted to leave with Dave Too, Dave jumped in the hood of his jacket and tried to leave with them both.

'Dave Too needs me,' Dave wailed, as a mad kerfuffle ensued with the Human Man trying to jostle Dave out of his clothing and the Human Lady trying to rescue him as he clung on to the hood like it was the last lifeboat in an ocean storm.

I didn't tell Dave that Dave Too seemed completely unbothered about leaving. It was probably because she'd developed a complete cat brain and truly didn't know what was going on because her head was full of air and bits of ear fluff.

With all the kittens safely in their new homes, Dave and I were back in our shed searching for stale crumbs just like Tinkles said we would.

And so we were back to our old ways of darting over to the Human Lady's house on daring adventures for mystery meals to eat in the great outdoors, with Mean Cat threatening us every pigeon step of the way because she wanted our incredible birdy company.

It didn't matter what life and death situation you had been through together, cats would always just be cats.

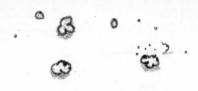

Apart from Dave Too.

Meow

127

Collect all of Dave and Skipper's adventures . . .

Cats beware! Dave and Skipper are writing a book about how they defeated Mean Cat in order to help fellow pigeons everywhere.

When their Human Lady goes on holiday, Dave and Skipper run out of food and have to find a new owner. But is Reginald Grimster all he seems? And why is he so keen on feeding them?

A trip to the pet shop to get Dave's wing fixed leads to a racing competition! Can Dave beat the evil Opprobrious Vastanavius the Parrot?

Dave swaps places with Prince Raju Pigeon, one of the Queen's personal birds from the Royal Lofts. But life in high society is not all it's cracked up to be . . .

Enjoy Lin's pandalicious adventures in the Bad Panda series!

Turn over to read an exclusive extract . . .

Are **YOU** sick of being utterly adorable?

Tired of being cuddled and hugged?

Fed up of having your head confused for your **bottom** because you just so happen to be SOOOOPER-DOOOOOPER fluffy?

Are you making plans to build a bamboo hut, with bamboo windows, bamboo shutters and a reinforced bamboo-laser door with bamboo cannons and catapults so you can fire panda poo at the next ranger who comes along and does those schmoopy-loopy-wubbie-schnubbie-gooey-heart eyes at you because they find you **'too cute, just too darn cute'?**

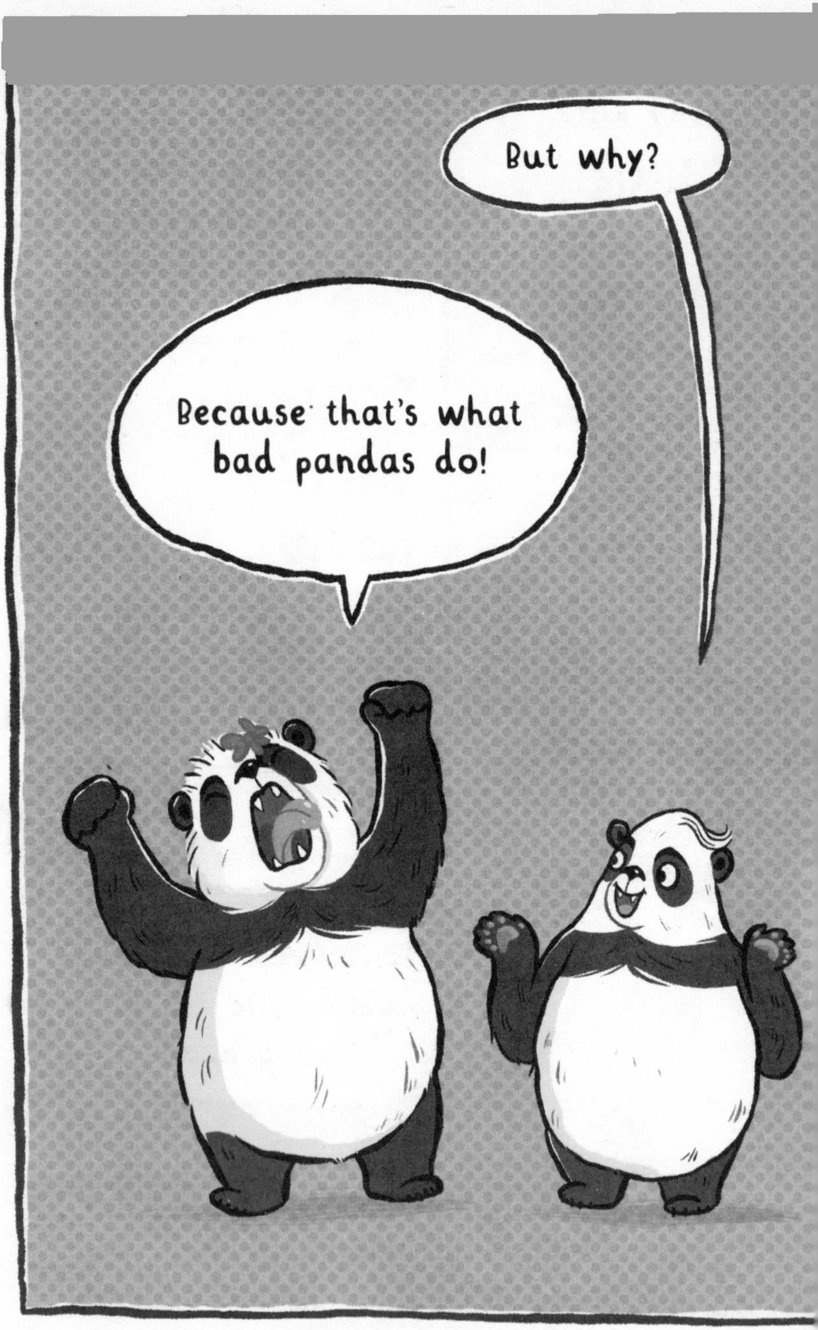
But why?
Because that's what bad pandas do!